*For you! Always know
that there's someone out there who cares.*

Henry Holt and Company, *Publishers since 1866*
Henry Holt® is a registered trademark of Macmillan Publishing Group, LLC
175 Fifth Avenue, New York, NY 10010 • mackids.com

ISBN 978-1-250-18589-1
Library of Congress Control Number 2018936453

Our books may be purchased in bulk for promotional, educational, or business use. Please contact your local
bookseller or the Macmillan Corporate and Premium Sales Department at (800) 221-7945 ext. 5442 or by
e-mail at MacmillanSpecialMarkets@macmillan.com.

First edition, 2018
The artist used pencil on paper and digital color in Adobe Photoshop to create the illustrations for this book.
Printed in China by RR Donnelley Asia Printing Solutions Ltd., Dongguan City, Guangdong Province

1 3 5 7 9 10 8 6 4 2

Merry Christmas, Little Elliot

Story and pictures by

Mike Curato

GODWINBOOKS

Henry Holt and Company 🍎 New York

Little Elliot was not excited about Christmas.

"Let's go see Santa," said Mouse.

"I want a toy train!" said Mouse.

In line, Elliot thought about what he wanted most.

"Can you give me the Christmas spirit?" Elliot asked Santa.

"I'm afraid I can't give that to you," said Santa. "You have to find that yourself."

"How do I find the
Christmas spirit?" asked Elliot.

"I don't know," said Mouse, "but I will help you look!"

Elliot and Mouse looked for the Christmas spirit at a show.

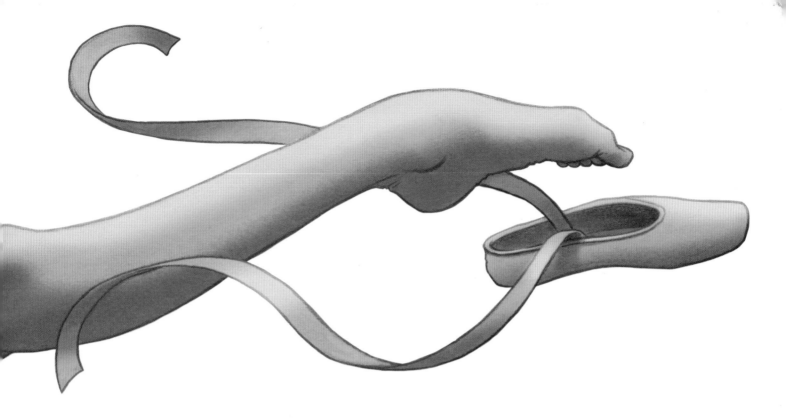

They went to see
a beautiful tree.

They even went sledding in the park.

"Have you found the Christmas spirit yet?"
asked Mouse.

"No," said Elliot. "Not yet."

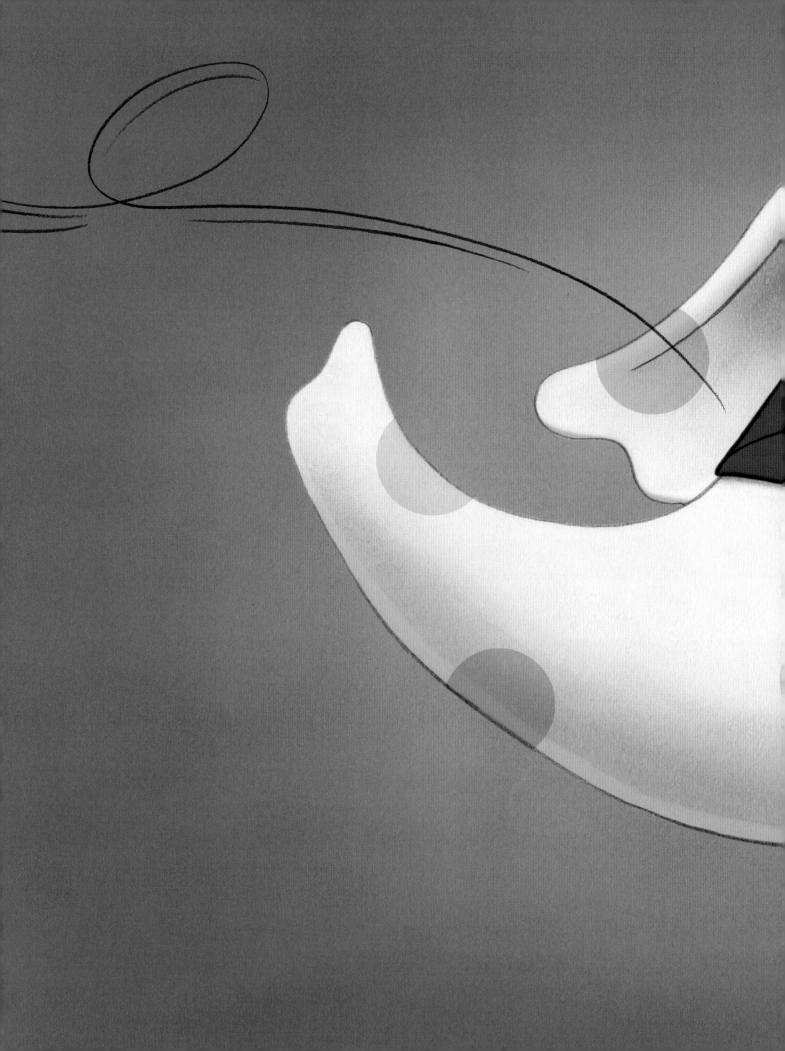

"Oh dear," said Elliot.

"We need to deliver this right away!"

The two friends rushed back,
but the long line was gone—
and so was Santa.

Elliot opened the letter.

"I wish we could help," he said.

He thought for a
moment about what
he should do . . .

"Let's go!" Elliot said.

Elliot and Mouse drove
through the night.

Finally, they arrived.

"MERRY CHRISTMAS!"
said Elliot and Mouse.

"We got your letter," said Mouse.

"And we're here to deliver
your gift," said Elliot.

At last, Elliot had found his Christmas spirit.